Fiddle Dancer

Li Daanseur di Vyaeloon

It was way past bedtime on New Year's Eve, but *Nolin's* shoes were still tapping.

Aashay kii kapishkamwuk chi nipaachik la vey di zhoor di laan, maaka Nolin avik sii sooyii kiiyapit taakishkikew.

The lively fiddle music gave him energy. He hopped from side to side, copying the other dancers.
Nolin glanced up and *Moushoom* winked from across the dance circle. Nolin tried even harder to get the step right.

La bonn musuk di vyaeloon oopiiyikoo. Ka kwaashkwatew aen borr a lootr, aen naashpitoohtawat lii danseur.
Nolin apanapew pi mooshoom chiipiikwaeyew iita ka niimiihk daan li cirrk di daans. Kwaatapwew Nolin koochiiew nawut lii boon stepp chi ooshitaat.

Then the tempo went faster. Moushoom moved to the middle to show off his fancy steps. The other dancers hooted and clapped. Moushoom's feet flashed high, then snapped the floor. The fringes on his sash bounced to the beat.

Pi nawut la musuk kishiipayin. Mooshoom daan li mijeu ishi niimew chi waapatayiwet sii boon stepp. Lii zootr danseur shakoowewuk pi leu maen pakamahamuk. Mooshoom shooki shooshkewpinikew pi li plaanshii mamatwehum. Lii fraansh daan sa saenchur flayshii ooshchi niimiishtamyew la musuk.

When the music slowed, Moushoom was gasping for breath. "I'm too old for this," he puffed.

Moushoom's friend yelled, "Hey, ol' *Baptiste*, better teach your grandson to take your place." Nolin felt his face turning red. He could never dance like Moushoom.

La musuk ka nakiimakak, Mooshoom la mizaer aen pakatatamoot ka ooshchi niimit ooshchi. "Jhi troo vyeu poor ooma itwew aen kipatatuhk."

Mooshoom sii zaamii taepwatikoo, "Hey, li vyeu Baachis, nawut chi kishkinahamwut kooshishim ta plass chi ootinamash." Nolin mooshitow soon vizaezh roozh aen kwaeshkipaniyik. Zhamae ka niimew tapishkoot mooshoom.

3

When the fiddlers stopped between tunes, Nolin squeezed Moushoom's hand. "I'm tired now."

Moushoom nodded. "Go sleep on my parka." He ruffled Nolin's hair. "Soon you'll know the fancy steps, my boy."

"No chance!" thought Nolin, as he wrapped himself in Moushoom's coat. He snuggled under a bench.

Lii zhooweur di vyaeloon ka nakiichik enn chune, Nolin maamakoonamwew omooshooma sa maen iyihk. "Dayaeshkooshin ooma la."

Mooshoom nanaamishkwayyiw. "Doo nipaa dissu moon parka." Sii zhveu wayyashkumwew. "Moon pchi garsoon wiiput lii boon stepp ka kishkayten."

"Nimoowiikaat!" tayhtum Nolin, aen waawaekinishoot daan omooshooma soon kapooiyihk. Kii shayshkooshin aan soor li baan.

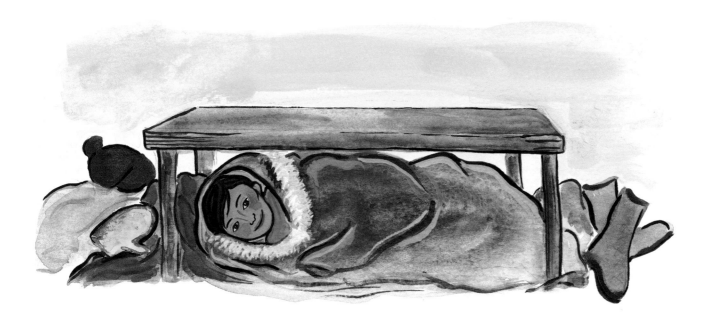

4

Big feet danced past him, shuffling, tapping, and kicking. Huge feet wearing leather shoes, or moccasins, or just plain ol' socks. Even a sock with a toe sticking out!

Lii groo pyii kapishkakoo, leu pyii pimitapaewuk, pakamahamwuk, takishkatamuk. Lii groo pyii lii sooyii di chwiir aen kishkatkihk, o baen lii soyii moo, o baen yaenk lii baa, ahpoo aen baa avik li zaartay aen shaakipayik!

5

As he fell asleep, Nolin felt the wooden floor bouncing to the beat of the dancers' feet.

Aen maachi nipaat, Nolin li plaanshii mooshitow lii danseur aen matwewtahtachik.

6

Nolin opened his eyes and sat up. This wasn't his bedroom!
Then he remembered. He was visiting Moushoom for New Year's.
Together they had gone to the community dance. Moushoom must
have carried him home.

The bedroom door squeaked as Nolin pushed it open.
Moushoom was reading in his old willow rocking chair.

"Good morning, my boy. I just woke up, myself. All that
dancing wore me out."

Nolin toohkapew pi chiipatapew. Nimooya ooma sa shaambr
ka nipaat! Kishkishoopayew. Aen kiiwooket si mooshoom poor
li zhoor di laan. Kii itootaywuk la daans daan la vill. Mooshoom
apootikwew kii nayoomikoo aen kiiwaychik.

La port di shaambr paytakoopayin, Nolin kayahkinahk.
Mooshoom amishchikew daan sa vyay shayz barseuz aan sool.

"Taanshi kiiya a matin, moon pchi gaarsoon. Aykwayak ooma
niishta aen ki kooshkopayiyan. La daans gii ayeshkooyikoon!"

"How did you learn to be such a good dancer, Moushoom?" asked Nolin.

Moushoom chuckled, "Got dancing in my bones, *Nooshishim*. You know how the dancing got in my bones?" Nolin shook his head.

"I'll tell you while I make us some bannock."

"Mooshoom taanshi ka ooshchi kishkaytamun aen ishi nita niimiyen." Mooshoom paapew, "La daans ashtew daan mii zhoo, Nooshishim. Kikishkayten taanshi la daans daan mii zhoo ka ayayaan chiin?" Nolin sa tet nihkwapinum.

"Ka wiitamatin payshkish aen la galettikayaan."

8

Moushoom groaned as he stood up. "Ooh..., I'm stiff today. I'm getting old." He pushed more logs into the cast-iron stove. "You know, your grandma and I danced all night when we were young. She was the best jigger in the North and the most beautiful Métis girl, too."

Mooshoom mah pinew ka niipatt. "Ooh...moon korr shiitawow anoosh. Ni maachi kaawikikaan." Li bwaa akinum daan soon pwel di ferr. "Ki kishkayten, koohkoom pi niiya toot la nuitt gii niiminaan maana ka li jeunwiiyaak. Sitae li miiyeur jiggeur daan li norr pi mina la pleu bel fii Michif."

For a moment Nolin felt an ache of sadness because *Koohkoom* had died last year. He missed her a lot.

Achiyow Nolin kii kaashkaytum akooz ookoomaa aen kii niipooyit lannii passii. Miitoni mishchet ki kaashkaymew.

Moushoom got out a big bowl. He poured in a heap of flour and a shake of baking powder. After he cut in some lard, he added water, and stirred. He dumped the dough on the table, and kneaded it with his strong hands.

Moushoom patted the dough down on a baking tray and poked it with a fork. "Did you know that Koohkoom was the best bannock maker in the North?"

"Now you are, Moushoom," said Nolin.

Mooshoom soon groo plaa kii natum. La farinn kii shiikinew pi li baking powder ki piwaynum. Apray atiht li saendoo ka manishuhk, kii takoonum dloo, pi kii atayhum. Kii shiikwaypinew sa path sur la tabb, pi kii mamakoonew avik sii groos maen forr.

Mooshoom kii mamakoonew la path sur aen nifripp pi ki chiistawew avik enn foorshett. "Ki kishkayten chiin koohkoom nawut aen kii nita la gallettikayt daan li norr?"

"Kiishkootum Mooshoom," itwew Nolin.

Moushoom slid the tray into the oven then eased back into his rocker.

"Tell me how dancing got in your bones," prompted Nolin.

"Well, it started even before I was born. Whenever *Ma Mayr* heard fiddle music, she drummed her fingers on her big belly. That beat vibrated inside her where I was curled up, waiting to be born. The jigging beat just soaked into my soft, little baby bones."

Nikaan Mooshoom ki ahkinum lifripp daan li foornoo pi kiitwaam ki apiw daan sa shaez di baarseus.

"Wiitamowin taanayki ka maachi nimiiyen," mina Nolin kaakwaychimew oomooshooma.

"Gii maachinimin avaan chi nitawakiyaan. Maamaa la musuk di vyaeloon ka payhtuk si dwae ki matwayhum sur soon groo vaantr. Ka matwayikaet sur soon vaantr gii payten iita ka waakishiyan aen payhooyaan chi nitawakiiyaan. La jig ka paytamaan kii ishpayin daan ma poo aen yooshkaak, pi mina mii pchi zhoo di baybii."

13

"Here, I'll show you." Moushoom caught Nolin in his strong arms. Before Nolin could squirm away, Moushoom swept the boy onto his lap. He tapped a frisky rhythm on Nolin's tummy…. 'Dum-diddley-diddley-dum…'

"Oooh, that tickles!" Nolin squealed. He snuggled against Moushoom's flannel shirt and breathed in its smoky-wood smell. They rocked back and forth.

Finally Moushoom spoke. "Know what happened after I was born?" Nolin shook his head.

"Chiwayr, ka wapatayitin." Mooshoom taypipitew Nolin avik si groo braa forr. Avaan Nolin chi tapashiit, Mooshoom ayikoo seu si ginoo. Kitooshchikaynakamoo payshkish pakamawew daan Nolin so vaantiyew … 'Dum-diddley-diddley-dum…'

"Oooh, nikyaykishin!" Nolin taypwew. Mooshoom sa shmiizh di flanalet kii shinikooshin pi payshkish pakatatamoo daan la bookaan di bwaa aen miiyatuhk. Too li deu kii wawaypishoowuk.

Piiyish Mooshoom piikishkwew. "Ki kishkayten chiin taanishi ka ishpayiyan apray ka nitawakiiyaan?" Nolin nikikwaypinum sa tet.

15

"My soft baby bones were full of music. Whenever I heard a fiddle on the radio I wanted to dance. I'd cry and cry until Ma Mayr picked me up and danced a jig. Then I was happy again."

"Ka li baybiiwiiyaan mii zhoo kii mooshkinaywa avik la musuk. Ka paytamaan li vyaeloon daan li raygiyoo shaymaak gii nootay niimin. Gii matoon zheusk ka taan ni maamaa aen mooshakinit pi enn jig aen niimit. La miina gii miyeusten."

Moushoom sniffed the air. "*Oyhoy, Nooshishim,* the bannock's gonna burn!"

Moushoom quickly opened the creaking oven door. Through a blast of heat, Nolin saw the golden brown bannock. Just perfect.

Moushoom picked up the bannock. "Ow, ow! *Kishitayw!*" he hollered, juggling the hot bread and hopping to the table.

Nolin giggled. "Is that the bannock jig, Moushoom?"

"Hey, I just invented a new fancy step!"

Mooshoom miyashchikew. "Oyhoy, Nooshishim, la gallett ka mayshchishoo!"

Mooshoom kakwayahoo aen yootaenuk la port di foornoo aen paytakwuk. Daan la klayrtii di shaleur, Nolin waapamew la gallett dorii shakwala. Mitooni kwayesh.

Mooshoom mooshakinew la gallett. "Ow, ow! Kishishoo!" taypwew, oohpinew la gallett shoo pi oopikwashkwatew daan la tabb taykay.

Nolin paapiikashoo. "La jig di gallett chiin anima Mooshoom?"

"Hey wii aen nootr stepp ooma ka ooshtayaan."

Nolin broke off a steaming chunk of bannock, dipped it in *Rogers Golden Syrup* and stuffed it into his mouth. Moushoom bit into another piece. "Mmm, almost as good as Koohkoom used to make."

"What happened next?" Nolin asked between bites.

Nolin paakwaypitew aen morsoo di gallett shoo, pi akooshchimew daan li siiroo pi mooshkinatow ootoonihk. Mooshoom enn booshii ki ootinum avik aen nootr morsoo. "Mmm, kaykaat paray taapishkoot Nookoom ka kii ooshihaat sa gallett."

"Taanishi ka ishpayihk mina?" Nolin kwaychimew maykwat aen aakummiichishoot.

"Pretty soon I could walk by myself," remembered Moushoom. "Whenever Ma Mayr heard jigging music on the radio, she held me so I could balance my little moccasins on her shoes. I soaked up the rhythm from her tapping feet."

"Wiiput gii payakootaan," aen kishkishiht Mooshoom. "Pikooshpii ni maamaan li jig ka paytuhk daan li raygiyoo, gii mishchiminik miisooyiimoo chi akotayki seu sii sooyii. Gii chiikiten la musuk si pyii ooshchi."

Nolin asked, "Is it too late to get dancing in *my* bones?"

Moushoom's eyes twinkled. "You're my grandson, aren't you? You just gotta learn the steps."

"We need music to get our bones moving. Here's a good CD, John Arcand. He's the best Métis fiddler around!"

An easy rhythm filled the air and Moushoom's feet started moving.

Nolin kakwaychimew, si troo taar chiin niishta la daans daan mii zhoo chi ayayaan?"

Mooshoom si zyeu niimiimashtayiw si koom lii zitwel. "Nooshishim kiiya chiin ooma? Chi kakway kishkaytaman lii stepp."

"Sa praan la musuk kishpin tii zhooynaan chi mamashchipayiki. Ooma aen boon CD, John Arcand aen kitooshchikayt. Wooya payek li miiyeur Michif aen kitooshchikayt li vyaeloon oota alaantoor!"

Kaytahtaway la musuk ka mooshkinayk daan la maezoon pi Mooshoom sii pyii ka mahtinuk.

"Stand on my feet, Nooshishim, and we'll dance together."

Nolin wrapped his arms around Moushoom's waist and held tight. He could feel Moushoom's tapping feet, his panting breath, and his pounding heart.

"Sur mi pyii niipawi, Nooshishim, pi aansaambl ka niiminaan."

Nolin shooki ooshchiminew omooshooma daan sa saenchuriyew. Mooshitawew omooshooma sii pyiiyew, aen pakatatamoot, pi soon koer aen shookaykotayihk.

Then Nolin's feet slipped off and his arms let go. But it didn't matter. He had the rhythm! Nolin danced to the end of the tune.

The tempo changed to the frisky beat of "Big John McNeil".

"Let's learn some fancy jig steps, my boy. Then we can both show off after dinner tonight," said Moushoom.

Pi Nolin sii pyii shooshkoopayinew pi sii braa pakichwaypinum. Maaka nimoonadow. La miin di musuk kii ayow! Nolin kii nimew juskataan la chune aen poonipayik.

Too daen koo mayshkochipayin la musuk "Big John McNeil" shipwaypinamuk.

"Niimiitak piitoosh lii step di jig moon pchi gaarsoon. Pi apray jhinii aswayr ka wapitayiwanaan aen ishi niimiyak," itway Mooshoom.

"Here's the 'Chi Galop'. One foot
in front of the other. Right, left, **right**.
Left, right, **left**.   Step, step, **step**."
    Nolin tried to copy but his feet
got all tangled up. "This is too hard!" he
hollered.

"Ooma li 'Pchi Galoo'. Aen pyii divan
lootr. A drwayt, goosh, a drwayt. Goosh,
drwayt, goosh, stepp, stepp, stepp."
    Nolin kakway naashpitotawew maaka
sii pyii tapishkoot aen tahkoopitayik. Si
troo jheur taypwew.

Moushoom turned off the music. "You can do it. Stand behind me." He danced in slow motion, leading with the right foot. Nolin copied. Moushoom repeated, leading with the left foot. He stopped and watched Nolin dance alone.

"Good work, my boy. Only one thing missing." Moushoom pulled his sash from the coat hook and wrapped it around Nolin's waist. "This will help your feet go faster."

Mooshoom nakiinum la musuk. "Ka kaashkitaan. A naaryayr niiya niipawi." Kii chakishimoo, niikaniw avik soon pyii drwayt. Nolin nashpitootahwew. Mooshoom kakiitwum-mishimoo, niikaniw avik soon pyii goosh. Kii nakiiw pi kanawapamew Nolin aen payakoshimoot.

"Ki nita niimin moon pchi garsoon. Yaenk payek piikoo ki patahen." Mooshoom sa saenchur flayshii niitinum daan li kroshet di capeau ooshchi pi pahkkotaywew Nolin wa. Ooma ka wiichihiyikoon tii pyii chi kishiipayiki.

Moushoom played "Big John McNeil" again. Together they danced the "Chi Galop" as fast as the fiddle played. Nolin's sash bounced to the beat.

The next tune started. Moushoom stopped to catch his breath, but Nolin kept stepping it out.

Mooshoom kitooshchikew mina "Big John McNeil". Kii niishooshimoowuk tapishkoot aen "Pchi Galoo aen miichshahakik li vyaeloon. Nolin kwashkwayshimoo avik sa saenchur flayshii pi la musuk.

Loot la chune kii maachipayin. Mooshoom nakiiw chi myeu pakatatamoot, maaka Nolin kiitwamishimoo.

"Look, Moushoom, your sash is making my feet fly."

"Chwayr Mooshoom ta saenchur flayshii ni wiichihiyikoon chi oopiiyaan avik mii pyii."

Moushoom joined in. He showed Nolin the "cross-step" and the "bunny step". Nolin caught on without missing a beat. When John Arcand burst into the rollicking rhythm of the "Red River Jig", Nolin was ready. He showed off three fancy steps while Moushoom hooted and clapped.

Mooshoom wiitchimooshtakoo. Kii kishkinamawew chi niimiyit
aen kashkamoonimit pi mina taapishkoot aen lyayv ka ishinimit. Nolin
shaymak tapwayeshkum, mahpoo paatahum la musuk. John Arcand ka
maachi kiitooshchikayt "la jig di la Rivyar roozh", Nolin parii ki ayow.
Kii nimew trwaa lii boon stepp maykwat Mooshoom aen shakoowet pi si
maen aen pakamahuk.

Suddenly, Moushoom exclaimed, "Nooshishim, look at the time! We gotta get going! It's a long drive and we don't want to be late for New Year's dinner."

Pulling on his boots, Nolin grinned. "I can't wait to show my mom!"

"Soon, you'll be the best jigger in the North," Moushoom said proudly.

"Not for a long time, Moushoom. You're the best jigger in the North and the best Grandpa, too."

Shishikut Mooshoom itway, "Nooshishim, chwayr leur. Sa praan chi shipwaytaeyaak waayow chi shpishooyaak pi nimoo anritaar chi ayayaak chi miichishooyak poor jhoor di laan."

Aen piishchpituk si sooyii Nolin paapinakooshew. "Jhakachipayhoon ni maamaa chi wahpatahuk!"

"Wiiput kiiya li miiyeur jiggeur daan li norr," Mooshoom kishchii-itaymoo aykooshishi aytikoot. "Kinwayshiish kiiyapit Mooshoom. Kiiya ooma li miiyeur jiggeur daan li nor pi mina li miiyeur Mooshoom."

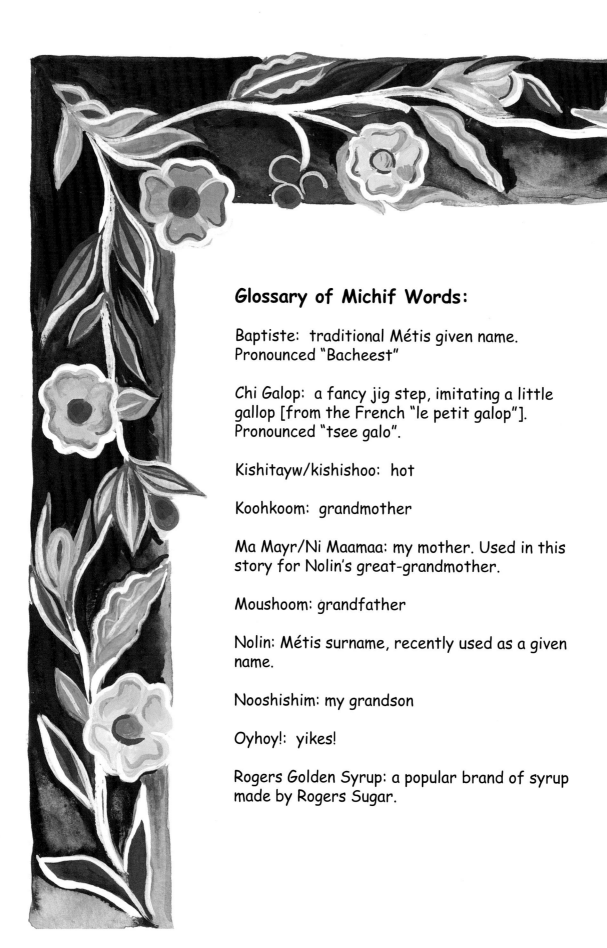

Glossary of Michif Words:

Baptiste: traditional Métis given name. Pronounced "Bacheest"

Chi Galop: a fancy jig step, imitating a little gallop [from the French "le petit galop"]. Pronounced "tsee galo".

Kishitayw/kishishoo: hot

Koohkoom: grandmother

Ma Mayr/Ni Maamaa: my mother. Used in this story for Nolin's great-grandmother.

Moushoom: grandfather

Nolin: Métis surname, recently used as a given name.

Nooshishim: my grandson

Oyhoy!: yikes!

Rogers Golden Syrup: a popular brand of syrup made by Rogers Sugar.

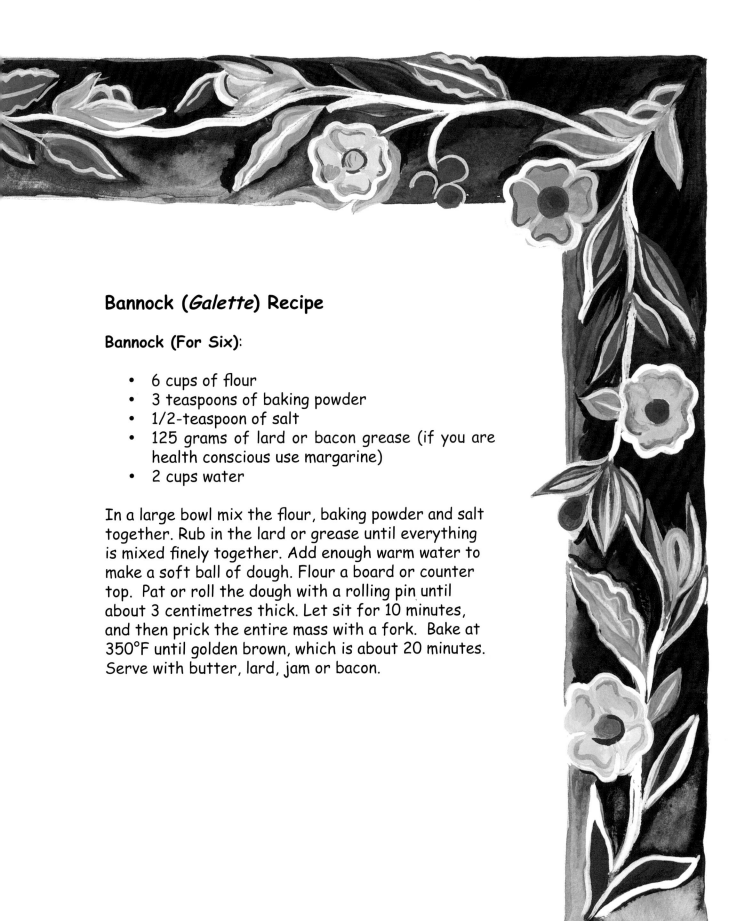

Bannock (*Galette*) Recipe

Bannock (For Six):

- 6 cups of flour
- 3 teaspoons of baking powder
- 1/2-teaspoon of salt
- 125 grams of lard or bacon grease (if you are health conscious use margarine)
- 2 cups water

In a large bowl mix the flour, baking powder and salt together. Rub in the lard or grease until everything is mixed finely together. Add enough warm water to make a soft ball of dough. Flour a board or counter top. Pat or roll the dough with a rolling pin until about 3 centimetres thick. Let sit for 10 minutes, and then prick the entire mass with a fork. Bake at 350°F until golden brown, which is about 20 minutes. Serve with butter, lard, jam or bacon.

About the Authors

Wilfred Burton, originally from the area around Glaslyn, Saskatchewan, is the son of Fred Burton and Georgina Nolin. He has been a teacher since 1979. His first elementary teaching position was in La Loche, Saskatchewan. He then taught for many years for the Regina Public School Board. He is currently a faculty member at the Saskatchewan Urban Native Teacher Education Program (SUNTEP) in Regina where he teaches pre-service teachers courses in reading, language arts, cross-cultural education, and children's literature. He is a graduate of the University of Regina, Saskatchewan Indian Federated College and the University of Victoria. Reading and jigging are his two loves. His first book *Fiddle Dancer* combines these two passions!

Anne Patton, originally from southern Ontario, she has lived in Saskatchewan for over forty years. Her teaching experiences include kindergarten, special education, primary and middle grades. To celebrate her retirement as an elementary school teacher, she backpacked throughout Southeast Asia with her daughter. Since returning, she has worked at SUNTEP instructing Métis education students. She has long been frustrated by the scarcity of children's literature reflecting life in Saskatchewan. She decided to tackle that problem by writing children's books.

Norman Fleury, originally from St. Lazare, Manitoba, is a gifted Michif oral storyteller. He has worked extremely hard in the promotion and preservation of Michif, including the production of language resources and an introductory Michif dictionary. He has been active with the Manitoba Métis Federation since 1967 and is currently its Michif Language Program Director. Married with two children, he farms southwest of Virden, Manitoba in the small community of Woodnorth.

Sherry Farrell-Racette is one of the early builders of the Gabriel Dumont Institute (GDI). During her tenure with GDI – as an educator, author and illustrator – she left an endurable legacy of highly-acclaimed resources, including *The Flower Beadwork People*, *The Flags of the Métis*, and several posters. She has also illustrated Maria Campbell's *Stories of the Road Allowance People* and Freda Ahenakew's *Wisahkecahk Flies to the Moon*. She recently completed her doctorate in traditional Métis clothing and adornment through the University of Manitoba.

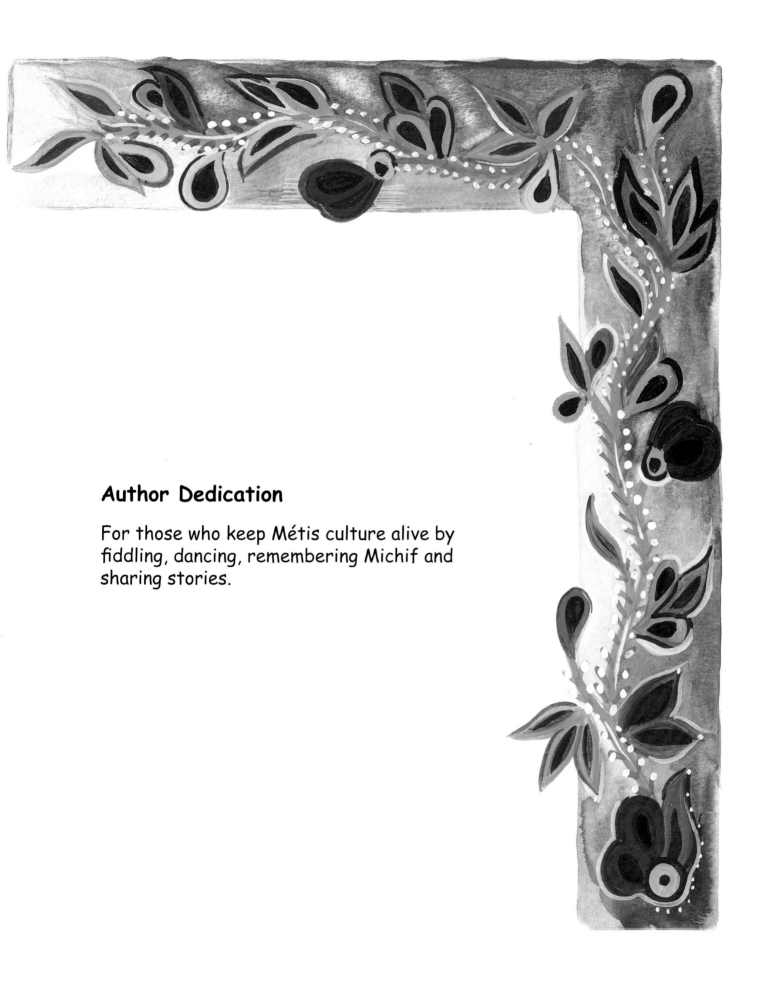

Author Dedication

For those who keep Métis culture alive by fiddling, dancing, remembering Michif and sharing stories.